TOO MANY PETS

An Edda Melkorka Story About Lice

Written by **Catherine Wayne and Robyn Phaedra Mitchell**

Illustrated by **Cindy Strosser**

For Edda Melkorka, a most amazing girl!

Edda Melkorka lives in Iceland.

Edda has a very nice cat named Brutus, but she wanted another pet.

One day before school, Edda asked, "Mom, can I have another pet?"

"What kind of pet do you want to get?"

"I would like a tiger," said Edda.

"A tiger would probably eat Brutus," explained Mom.

"How about a zebra?" suggested Edda.

"A zebra is too big to keep in the house," said Mom.

Edda explained, "But he could live in the backyard and eat grass."

"He'd still be too big for our backyard."

"Oh crud," said Edda. "What about a turtle?"

Mom shook her head. "A turtle would need a pond to live in and we don't even have a bathtub."

"Rats a la mode!" said Edda. "What about a bird?"

Mom thought for a moment then said, "Brutus likes to eat birds. I don't think a bird would last as a pet."

Edda was beginning to think that she would never get another pet.

The next day when Mom picked Edda up from school, she got a letter. The letter said lice had been found and some might go home with the students. Parents had to comb their kids' hair every night and use special shampoo to get the lice out.

"Oh no," said Mom. "I guess we need to comb your hair tonight to see if you have lice."

"Okay," said Edda. "Mom, what is a lice?"

Mom explained, "Not 'a lice' Edda. One is called a louse and more than one are called lice. It's like mouse and mice."

"Oh, I get it. So what is a louse?" Edda asked.

"It's a little bug that likes to live in your hair and make your head itch."

Edda was very interested in these animals.
"Do lots of kids have lice?"

"Yup. Lice seem to like kids a lot."

Edda wondered if lice would make good pets.

Mom combed Edda's hair but did not find any lice. Edda was disappointed.

The next day at school, Edda heard that some of her friends had lice and on the way home from school Edda's head felt a bit itchy.

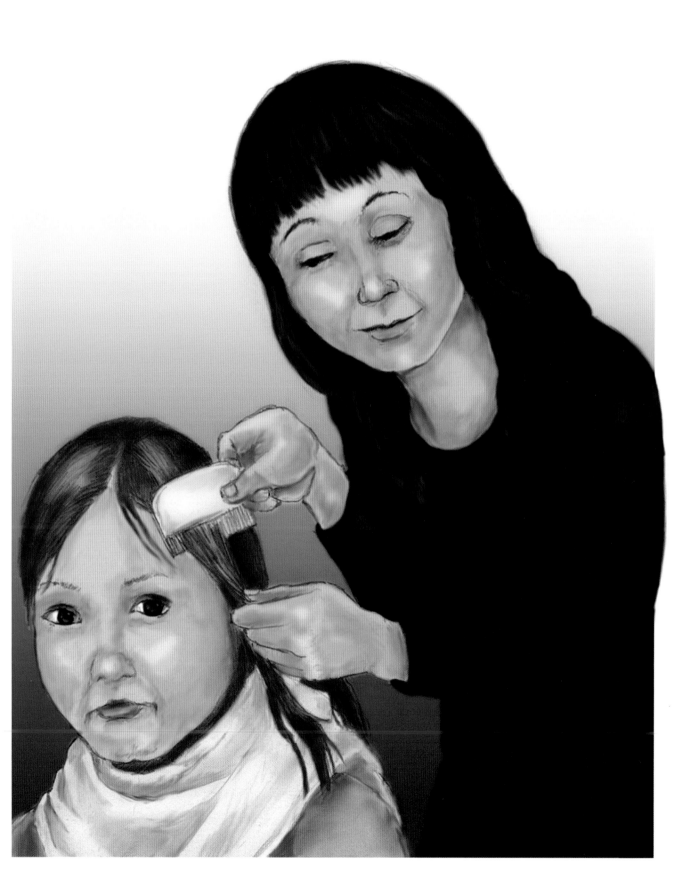

After supper, Edda sat quietly while Mom combed her hair. The combing hurt a bit but it was worth it because after a while Mom cried, "AHA! Edda I found a louse in your hair!"

Edda was very excited. "Mom, please give me a little box that can be a house for my louse. I'm going to name him Hoppy."

Mom gave Edda a look.

Edda sighed. "I guess I will have to find my own little box."

Edda put Hoppy in the little box and said, "Maybe I will find some friends for you tomorrow."

The next day, Edda's head was itchy all day long. That night, Edda sat quietly while Mom combed her hair. The combing hurt quite a bit but this time, Mom found two more lice. "I will call them Scratchy and Fred," said Edda. She put Scratchy and Fred in the little box with Hoppy.

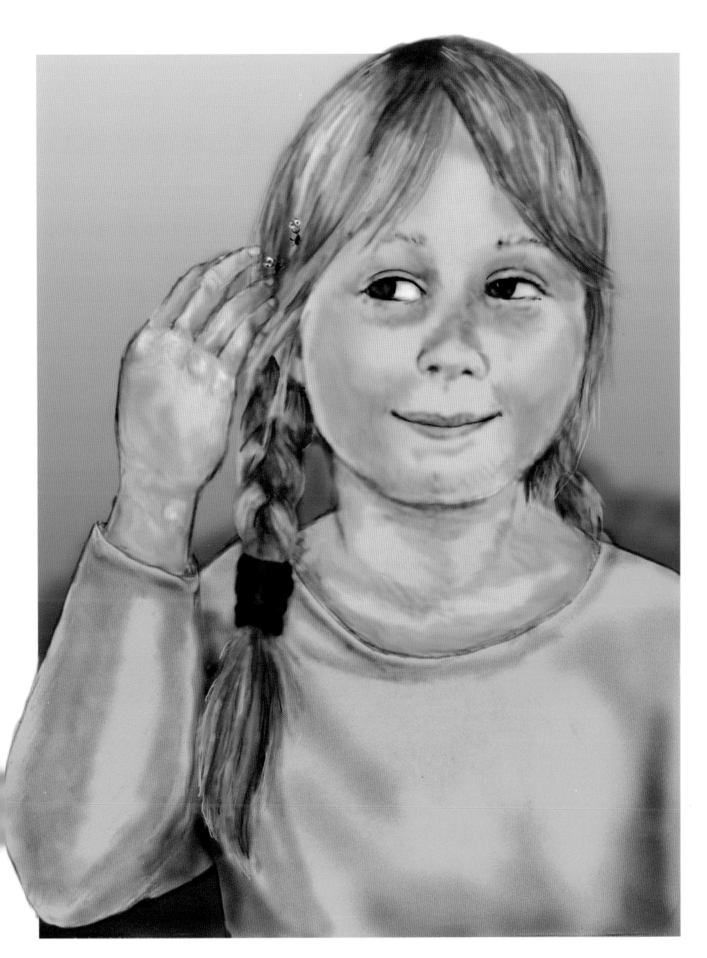

The next day, the same thing happened. Only this time, Mom found seven lice. "Hmmmmmmm…" said Edda. "I need seven new names." Edda remembered Grampa telling her that Earth was just one of the planets in our solar system. There were seven other planets. So, she named the newcomers Mercury, Venus, Mars, Jupiter, Saturn, Uranus, and Neptune. When Edda put her newest pets into the little box, she noticed that the little box was getting quite crowded so she asked Mom for a bigger box.

Mom gave Edda a look.

Edda sighed. "I guess I will have to find my own bigger box." Edda moved all her lice to a bigger box.

At school the next day, Edda's head was very itchy. Again, Edda sat quietly while Mom combed her hair even though it hurt a lot. This time, Mom found thirteen lice. "Now I need thirteen more names," said Edda.

Edda thought and thought about what to name the new lice. Then she remembered there are thirteen Icelandic Yule Lads, so she named her new pets Sheep Worrier, Gully Gawk, Stubby, Spoon Licker, Pot Scraper, Bowl Licker, Door Slammer, Skyr Gobbler, Sausage Swiper, Window Peeper, Door Sniffer, Meat Hook, and Candle Stealer. Edda put her new pets into the bigger box. *That bigger box is getting very crowded*, thought Edda.

"Mom," she said, "I need an even bigger box."

Mom gave Edda a look.

Edda sighed. "I guess I will have to find my own even bigger box." Edda moved all her pets to the even bigger box.

Soon, Edda's head was very, very itchy. She wondered if she was getting too many pets. Edda decided that she would not bring any more lice home from school.

"I do not want any more pets," Edda said to her head.

The lice did not listen.

That night, Edda cried when Mom combed her hair because Mom had to comb and comb and comb and comb. By the time Mom finished combing, Edda had twenty more lice. *Where will I ever find twenty new names?* thought Edda. Edda asked Mom if she could use the computer and she went online and typed in "Twenty Names" because she needed twenty names.

Up popped a list of the volcanoes of Iceland. Edda thought she could name her new lice after the volcanoes. Some volcano names were easy to say, like Katla and Hekla, but some of the names were a bit harder like Eyjafjallajokull and Reykjaneshryggur.

Edda thought she had better come up with some names for her pets that would be easy to remember so she named them One, Two, Three, Four, Five, Six, Seven, Eight, Nine, Ten, Eleven, Twelve, Thirteen, Fourteen, Fifteen, Sixteen, Seventeen, Eighteen, Nineteen, and Twenty.

"Whew!" exclaimed Edda. "Naming all these pets is hard work."

When Edda went to put her new lice in the even bigger box, she realized that they would not all fit comfortably, so she said to Mom, "Mom, I need a great big box."

Mom gave Edda a look.

Edda sighed. "I guess I will have to find my own great big box." Edda moved all of her pets to the great big box.

"That's it! I have too many pets! I do not want any more pets. I have to figure out a way to make sure I don't get any more."

Edda went to Mom and asked, "Mom, how can I make sure I don't bring any more lice home?"

"Well," Mom said, "you would have to make sure that we comb your hair every night and use the special shampoo. And you would have to make sure that all the other kids comb their hair every day and use the special shampoo until all the lice are gone."

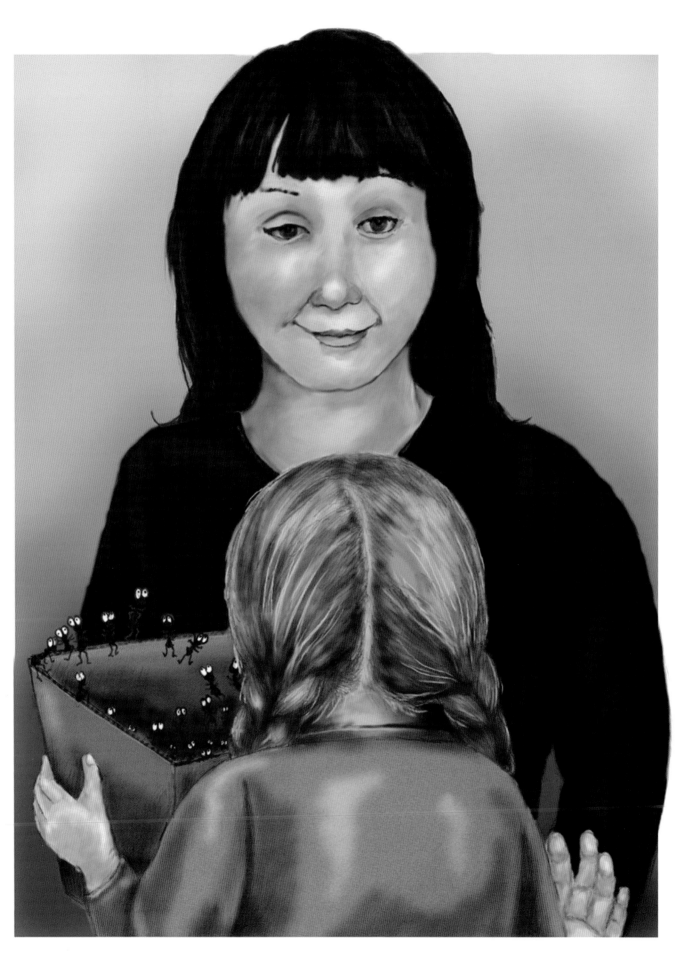

The next day, Edda went to school and said to her teacher, "I have an announcement to make to the whole school." Edda's teacher took Edda to the school office where there was a microphone.

Edda picked up the microphone. "I have TOO MANY PETS!" she said. "I have Hoppy, Scratchy, Fred, Mercury, Venus, Mars, Jupiter, Saturn, Uranus, Neptune, Sheep Worrier, Gully Gawk, Stubby, Spoon Licker, Pot Scraper, Bowl Licker, Door Slammer, Skyr Gobbler, Sausage Swiper, Window Peeper, Door Sniffer, Meat Hook, Candle Stealer, One, Two, Three, Four, Five, Six, Seven, Eight, Nine, Ten, Eleven, Twelve, Thirteen, Fourteen, Fifteen, Sixteen, Seventeen, Eighteen, Nineteen, and Twenty.

"I need to stop getting pets," Edda told the whole school. "There is only one way to be sure that I don't get any more lice. Everybody needs to make sure that they get their hair combed every night no matter what and that they use the special shampoo no matter what. My head is so itchy that if I get any more lice, I think my head will fall off."

All the kids at school scratched their heads as they listened to Edda. They had too many lice too.

That day, all the kids went home and said to their parents, "I need you to comb my hair every night no matter what and use the special shampoo no matter what."

The parents did just that, and after a few days the kids' heads were not so itchy.

After about three weeks, Mom did not find any more lice in Edda's hair.

"Yay!" shouted Edda. "No more lice!"

All the kids at school were very happy that the lice were gone.

Edda took the great big box outside and told all the lice to go away.

The lice were not very happy about it because they liked being Edda's pets, but they went away.

After all the lice were gone, Edda went and found Brutus.

Brutus was curled up on the end of the couch.

Edda picked up Brutus and cuddled him.

"Brutus," said Edda, "you're the only pet I need."

About the Authors

Catherine Wayne is a Canadian writer who lives on the West Coast of Canada and is, among other things, a Gramma. Robyn Phaedra Mitchell is her daughter, a Canadian who lives in Reykjavik, Iceland. Edda Melkorka is Robyn's daughter and Catherine's granddaughter. Catherine and Robyn write as a team.

About the Series

The Edda books are inspired by conversations between Gramma, Robyn, and Edda. The books are written in a style that is honest, age-appropriate, funny, and educational. These books feature adventures with family members and friends on both sides of the Atlantic Ocean, and they address learning about social issues, values, getting along, and other important life lessons. The level of reading is appropriate for readers ages six to nine.